# FAIRY TALES

Illustrated by
## VAN GOOL

Colour
Library
Direct

# CONTENTS

© Creation, text and illustrations: A.M. Lefèvre, M. Loiseaux, M. Nathan-Deiller, A. Van Gool.
Editorial direction: CND International, Paris.

Published and produced bij ADC International, 1997, Eke-Nazareth, Belgium.
CLD 20857. This edition printed in 1998 for Colour Library Direct, Godalming Business Centre, Woolsack Way, Godalming Surtey, GU7 1XW.
Printed in China.
ISBN 1 85833 825 5

"VAN GOOL'S"

# Jungle Book

It was a hot evening in the Indian jungle and Father Wolf was waking after a long nap. He was feeling hungry and deciding where to hunt when a visitor arrived: it was Tabaqui the jackal.

"Beware Father Wolf! Shere Khan, the big tiger, has changed his hunting ground. He stalks his prey here. Protect your children!"

And with that the jackal rushed off into the dense jungle.

Shere Khan appeared a few minutes later. The wolf family defended their territory, but in their anger had not noticed the human baby that was crawling behind them.

"That baby is mine!" snarled the tiger.

"No! This is our hunting ground – go away!" growled Father Wolf.

Shere Khan sauntered away, planning to get revenge at another time for the meal he had just been denied. When he was gone, the wolves looked at the man-child.

"We should look after this child," said Mother Wolf. "We will call him Mowgli."

"First we must ask the opinion of the Wolf council," said Father Wolf.

When Mowgli was brought before the council, Akela their chief asked, "Is it right that this man-child stays with us? Who here will protect him?"

An old bear, Baloo, was at the edge of the meeting, listening.

"I will teach Mowgli the law of the jungle, as I have taught your children," he suggested.

At the other side of the meeting the shadowy figure of Bagheera, the panther, was visible in the fading light.

"I will help Baloo to look after this child," she declared. And thus was Mowgli accepted by the wolf council and their people.

As the years passed Mowgli became strong and agile. The lessons from Baloo had taught him the ways of the jungle. He could swim and climb, he knew how to hunt to feed himself, and he knew the languages of all the animals around him. Mowgli was a good student.

Mowgli lived a carefree life, but all the time the wolves, Bagheera, and Baloo warned him of the dangers around him.

"Beware of Shere Khan, always," stressed Bagheera. "He is cunning and patient, and has vowed to take revenge . . ."

"Oh I know Bagheera! You're always telling me!" moaned Mowgli.

Baloo warned him about
the monkeys. They had no
laws, unlike the wolves, and
loved to play tricks.
"Don't talk to them!" he
cautioned.

The monkeys, however, were very interested in Mowgli. One day, as he dozed between his two friends, he felt lots of small hands lifting him into the air. "Come and have fun with us, little man," they chimed, as they pulled him up into the tree.

When Baloo and Bagheera woke up, they could not find Mowgli anywhere and were worried. The monkeys must have kidnapped him!

"Let's go and see Kaa," suggested Bagheera. "He knows what goes on in the trees, and he does not like the monkeys."

Kaa was in his usual sunny spot and welcomed them to his lair.

"I can lead you to where the monkeys are living," he hissed. "Follow me."

The monkeys had taken Mowgli to their hideaway, an old Indian town in ruins.

"Leave me alone!" wailed Mowgli as they pulled at his arms and legs, and tripped him up.

"No," cried the monkeys. "We're having fun!"

Suddenly there was a terrible roar and Bagheera was visible on the wall above them. Frantic, the monkeys threw Mowgli into a pit of snakes.

"I know your language," murmured Mowgli to the hissing mass, remembering his lessons from Baloo.

"We understand you and will not harm you," they replied.

A terrible fight broke out as Bagheera and Baloo tried to rescue Mowgli. There were too many monkeys for the two of them to fight. Baloo tossed them away, as they charged at him, but Bagheera was in trouble.

"Bagheera!" cried Mowgli. "Jump in to the water!"

The panther was relieved to hear Mowgli's voice above the screeching of the angry monkeys.

Suddenly Kaa uncoiled like a spring and pounced into the middle of the monkeys. To avoid him the monkeys jumped into an empty pit and were trapped.

"So this is young Mowgli," whispered Kaa when the fight had stopped. "He looks just like one of these monkeys."

"Thank you for rescuing me," said Mowgli politely.

"Now for my dinner," said Kaa. Hypnotized by the big snake, the monkeys were standing immobile in the pit. Bagheera and Baloo weren't feeling too well either . . . Mowgli took them home.

Then one night a few days later, the young wolves who admired Shere Khan for his strength, invited him to speak at their council.

"Mowgli, the wolves don't want you to stay anymore," he snarled. "You are a nuisance."

"Shere Khan, I'm not afraid of you!" cried Mowgli. "If my brothers want me to go then I will, but I will fight you first."

Mowgli decided to follow the advice of Bagheera after issuing the challenge to Shere Khan. He was going to steal fire from the human village. At the entrance of the village Mowgli saw a small boy carrying an earthenware pot full of ashes. Mowgli grabbed the pot and ran back to the jungle.

With a torch lit from the embers, Mowgli was able to successfully drive Shere Khan away. "He won't be gone for good, though," thought Mowgli, "and my brother wolves want me to leave. I am a danger to them more than ever now."

So Mowgli left his family of wolves and walked to the human village. He was hungry and dirty when he got there and could not understand the villagers. He looked like the wolves he had been living with and the villagers were afraid of his strange actions, and thought him mad.

Gradually though, the villagers grew used to Mowgli, and allowed him to tend their buffalo. He learned to speak their language, but thought their lives strange. He did not want to sleep in their houses. Mowgli still saw some of his friends; Grey Brother, a wolf, remained loyal and would visit with news about the jungle.

Mowgli wasn't unhappy living with the villagers, but he missed Baloo and Bagheera. He tried to adjust to their way of life, and to obey their laws. At nighttime they would gather to listen to the medicine man telling stories about the jungle, and Mowgli laughed at his ignorance. But there was one thing that frightened the villagers: Shere Khan.

One day when he met with Grey Brother, Mowgli asked his help to catch Shere Khan.

"Warn me when you know he is near."

"How will you catch him?" asked the wolf.

"I will use my buffalo . . ."

Not long after that meeting, Grey Brother came to warn Mowgli, "Shere Khan is sleeping nearby."

Together they herded the buffalo into the ravine, and surrounded the sleeping tiger. The buffalo, scenting the tiger, began to panic and before Shere Khan knew what was happening he was trampled by the buffalo. Mowgli sent the buffalo back to the village.

Mowgli set to work on the body of Shere Khan, and then rested the beautiful coat on a tree. The medicine man from the village came to see what Mowgli had done.

"You are only a shepherd, nobody will believe that you killed this mighty tiger. Give me the skin and I will show it to the village."

But Mowgli was suspicious of the medicine man. Grey Brother scared him away.

55

Mowgli was proud of what he had done; he had beaten his enemy with cunning and guile. He displayed the skin of Shere Khan to the villagers, but they threw stones at him.

"Get out!" they cried. "You're not human! Children don't kill tigers!"

Rejected by the humans, Mowgli returned to the jungle and displayed the skin of Shere Khan to the wolf council. His friends, Bagheera and Baloo, weren't surprised to see that he had succeeded. The young wolves were impressed, and they asked Mowgli to live among them again.

So again Mowgli lived and hunted with Bagheera, Baloo and the wolves. He had learned a lot living with the humans, and had grown into a man, but preferred life in the jungle with his friends.

# Beauty and the Beast

Once upon a time there lived a wealthy merchant who had three daughters. They lived a comfortable life in a mansion by the sea. While two of his daughters wasted their father's money on extravagant clothing, the youngest daughter, Beauty, helped the family as much as she could, dressing simply and working hard at her chores.

One day the daughters overheard gentlemen in the courtyard, saying that the merchant's ships had sunk in a storm. "He's got nothing left," said one of them, shaking his head, "he's ruined!"

To save his business and his fortune, the desperate merchant traveled the next day to a big city. He asked the bankers there if he could borrow the money, but the bankers refused.

Sadly, the merchant began his long trip home. He hardly noticed the falling snow as he thought about his daughters. As he had left to see the bankers, the eldest two had asked for jewels and gowns. Beauty had asked for a single rose.

The merchant forgot his dismay at not being able to fulfill his daughters' wishes, and his worry over his lost fortune, when the snowfall turned into a blizzard. Icy winds whipped snow at the merchant and his horse. Soon he was so lost that when a mysterious flying pixie appeared, and summoned him to follow, the merchant trailed along behind.

Just when the merchant was beginning to think he would freeze, the pixie shouted in a tiny, gruff voice, "Here! Come inside. We'll take care of you."

The merchant gazed in wonder at the enormous castle before him.

After he had settled his horse in the
barn with sweet hay, the merchant
followed the pixie into the castle.

"Come sit by the fire," chattered the
pixie. "You must be very cold, and
hungry."

As the merchant approached the table before the cheerfully blazing fireplace, he was amazed to see a sumptuous banquet appear in a twinkling of magic. "Eat!" exclaimed the pixie, chuckling at the man's surprise.

"Thank you so much for your kindness," said the merchant gratefully. He sat and ate until he could eat no more.

Then, feeling full and warm, the exhausted merchant fell asleep at the table. Even the pixie, warmed by the crackling fire, dozed off into a dreamless sleep. As they slept, a great hulking figure watched silently from the balcony.

In the morning the merchant awoke, refreshed, and again thanked the pixie for his hospitality.

"I must go home to my daughters," he said, thinking sadly of his troubles. As the merchant passed through the arch, he stared in wonder at a rose bush, blooming magically in the snow. The roses reminded him of Beauty's modest request, and he reached to pick one of the graceful flowers.

"No!" cried the pixie. But it was too late.

Suddenly an enormous Beast appeared. "Is this how you repay my kindness—by stealing my precious roses?" thundered the angry creature. "For this you shall die!"

"I-I'm sorry," stammered the merchant. "It was for my daughter."

"Your daughter?" replied the Beast gruffly. "If she loves you, she will come here to take your place. But if she does not, then you yourself must return within three months. Now go!"

The poor merchant promised to
return—what else could he do? Then
he rode home, his heart heavy with
sorrow.

But when he arrived at his home and
gave Beauty the rose, her happiness
cheered him. "Ah, Beauty," he said
ruefully. "If only you knew what this
rose cost." And he told his wondering
daughters his story about the Beast's
castle, and of the monster's terrible
demand.

"I will go in your place, Father!" cried Beauty. "I would rather be the Beast's prisoner than have you die for me."

"I'll hear no more of that!" replied the merchant firmly. "I shall return in three months."

Beauty's sisters glared angrily at her.

Three months passed quickly, and on the last morning, Beauty, carrying her shoes, quietly slipped out of the mansion.

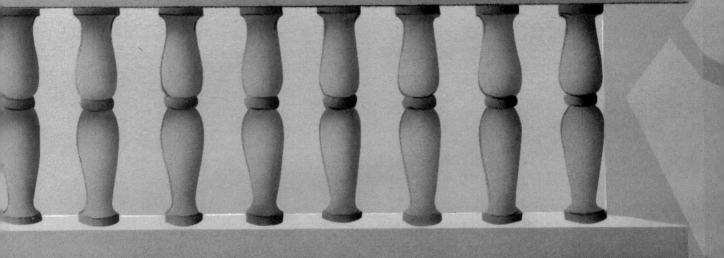

She saddled and mounted her
father's patient horse and bade a silent
farewell to her sleeping family. She
knew she would miss them terribly, but
felt strong in her resolve to save her
father's life.

"Besides," she thought
bravely. "Perhaps I can
change the Beast's mind."

Beauty arrived at the Beast's castle at nightfall, after the long journey. The pixie appeared as she entered the courtyard.

"Welcome, Beauty! Follow me . . . right this way," he exclaimed. He seemed to have been expecting her.

Beauty followed him into the castle.

The pixie led Beauty
through a maze of hallways to
a beautiful room filled with
roses and fine furniture.

"This is your bedroom!"
said the pixie. Then he
showed her a chest of
glittering jewels. "All these
are yours. A gift from my
master." He nodded
excitedly, then flew out the
door.

Beauty explored the room, gazing in wonder at the roses, the jewels, the furniture, the closet filled with beautiful clothing. She took off her simple traveling clothes and tried on an elegant gown.

Suddenly the pixie appeared again. "Oh, you look marvelous!" he sputtered. "My master will be so pleased. Just look at yourself in the mirror!"

Beauty gasped in horror. Behind her own reflection in the mirror, she saw the hideous Beast. She whirled around to face him.

"Welcome to my castle," said the Beast. "Have you come willingly?"

"Yes, I have," replied Beauty.

"You must be hungry after your long trip," he said hoarsely. "Come with me."

The Beast led Beauty to the enormous
living room, where a table had been set
for one. Although she felt relieved that
she wouldn't have to eat with the
frightful Beast, Beauty was touched by
his kindness. He bade her good-night,
and she ate her dinner. Then she stared
at the fire and thought about the Beast,
and this strange and magical castle.

The next night the Beast came to see Beauty as she wandered in the garden.

"Do you think I'm ugly?" he asked, leaning toward her.

"Yes," replied Beauty honestly. "But I think you are good."

"Would you marry me?" asked the Beast.

Startled by his unexpected question, Beauty answered, "no!"

Every day the Beast came to see Beauty, and they talked. She became less afraid of him, but when he asked her to marry him, as he did every night, her reply was always the same.

One day Beauty looked into the magic mirror in her bedroom, and saw her father. He was holding a picture of her, and he looked very sick.

Beauty ran to find the Beast. "You must let me go!" she cried. "Please, I know you are kind and good. My father is sick and needs me."

"Then go," said the Beast quietly. "But promise to come back before eight days have passed."

"I promise," whispered Beauty.

Beauty rode home as fast as her horse would go.

"Father!" she cried, hurrying into the mansion.

"Beauty! You are alive and well!" exclaimed her father, hugging her tightly. "The evil Beast didn't hurt you."

"No, Father," replied Beauty. "He's only a monster on the outside. Inside he is generous and sweet. But how are you?"

"I shall be fine, now that I know you are well," said her father, smiling.

The days passed quickly, and on the seventh night, the pixie came to Beauty while she was sleeping. He whispered in her ear, and Beauty dreamed that the Beast, forlorn and alone, waited for her, his desperate hope that she would return slowly fading.

In the morning, Beauty told her father and sisters that she must return to the Beast's castle, as she had promised. Her sisters, jealous of her fine gown and jewels, tried to keep her from going.

But Beauty waited until they were busy . . .

. . . then she slipped outside. "The Beast needs me," she thought. "I must go to him."

Beauty patted the horse's neck. "Run like the wind," she said to him. "I fear that the Beast is dying. He was kind to me, and he trusted me. I see now that beneath his ugliness, he has a special beauty."

The pair raced through the forest toward the Beast's castle.

When Beauty arrived at the castle, and couldn't find the Beast, she was frightened. "Beast!" she called. "Where are you?"

Then a tiny voice called, "This way, Beauty! Follow me." It was the pixie. Beauty followed him, and found the Beast lying in the courtyard.

"Beauty," he whispered. "I'm so happy to see you once more before I die."

"You can't die, Beast!" cried Beauty. She kneeled and kissed his cheek. "I love you," she whispered. "I want to marry you."

The Beast closed his eyes. Suddenly the courtyard was filled with a brilliant light. Magic filled the air.

Beauty looked in astonishment at the handsome Prince before her. "Where is my precious Beast?" she asked.

"Here he is," replied the Prince. "Your love has broken the evil spell that made me the Beast. I love you, Beauty."

"Your love has made me very happy," said Beauty, smiling.

"All this is ours to share," said the Prince, gesturing to the castle. Beauty knew her family would never be poor again.

Beautiful music filled the air as the two gazed at each other, thinking of the happiness they would share forever after.

# Puss in Boots

Once upon a time in a village in a kingdom, there lived a miller and his three sons. The miller's family always had enough to eat, but none to spare. One day, the old miller was so sick that he called his sons to his bedside.

"I have no fortune," said the miller. "But you may share what little I have."

The miller's only belongings were
his mill, his donkey and his cat. To
his oldest son he left his mill, and to
his middle son he left his donkey. To
his youngest son, the miller left his
cat. Then the old miller died.

While the youngest son was fond of the cat, he felt that his father had not dealt fairly with him, for his brothers could earn a living with a mill and a donkey, but it seemed that little fortune could be made with a cat. "I suppose you can catch mice," the young man said, scowling at the cat, "but what use is that?"

Suddenly, much to the young man's surprise, the cat spoke. "Look here," he said quite plainly. "Get me a fine hat, cape and boots, and I'll see that your fortune will be bright."

Astonished to hear the cat speak, the miller's son obeyed at once.

Taking his last coins, he went into the village and bought the clothes. The cat was very pleased when he slipped on the boots, hat and cape. Then he set off down the road, leaving his master to wonder if he'd been foolish to trust such an eccentric cat.

The cat, who soon came to be called Puss in Boots, stepped brightly along the road, until he came to a briar patch. There he lay down and pretended to be dead. Curious, a rabbit hopped out of the patch. Puss in Boots jumped up and seized it by the ears.

Puss in Boots marched directly to the king's palace, where he insisted on seeing the king at once.

Puss was escorted to the throne room, where he bowed deeply and presented the rabbit, saying, "Greetings, Your Majesty. My noble lord, the Marquis of Carabas, has sent me to deliver this gift to you personally, with special regards to the princess."

"Please give your master my thanks," said the king.

The next day Puss in Boots returned to the palace, presenting partridges to the king on behalf of his master. Again, the king was pleased with the gift. "The Marquis is a generous man," said the king.

Then, as Puss in Boots was leaving, he heard the king asking the princess if she was ready for their drive along the river.

Puss in Boots ran all the way back to his master, and instructed him to go at once to the river to bathe. When the young man questioned him, the cat said, "Trust me. Do as I say, and your future will be bright."

"Come now, hurry!" urged the cat. As they made their way to the river, Puss in Boots said, "Now, if anyone asks your name, tell them you are the Marquis of Carabas."

"Are you sure you know what you're doing?" asked the miller's son. Puss in Boots replied with a wink.

The young man took off his ragged clothes and left them on the riverbank. Then he dived into the river. "Ah! The water feels great, Puss. Are you coming in?"

Before the cat could reply, the royal carriage came rumbling past. "Help!" shouted Puss in Boots. "The Marquis of Carabas is drowning! Help!"

When the king heard the familiar name, he ordered that the young man be rescued. "Sire," the cat whispered to the king, so as not to embarrass the princess, "while my master was bathing, all his clothes were stolen."

Puss had cleverly hidden his master's clothes. The king ordered a servant to fetch one of his finest suits.

In no time, the young man was dressed in a royal outfit that made him look very handsome. "So you're the Marquis of Carabas!" called the king.

"I'm privileged to meet Your Majesty," replied the young man, bowing.

"Perhaps you'd like to join us for a ride in the country," offered the king. The young man climbed into the royal carriage, and they set off.

Puss in Boots rushed down the road
ahead of the carriage, until he came to a
forest, where he found some woodcutters.
"Listen here!" he shouted, brandishing his
sword. "The royal carriage will be here
shortly. When the king asks who owns
these woods, you must tell him they are
owned by the Marquis of Carabas, or
you will be severely punished."

Then Puss in Boots hurried farther down the road until he came to a large field that the peasants were reaping. "I am a royal messenger!" shouted the cat, as the peasants stopped to listen. "When the king passes by and asks who owns these fields, you must tell him they are owned by the Marquis of Carabas."

The peasants nodded agreement.

Soon, the royal party arrived and the king ordered the carriage to stop. "Who owns these fields?" he called to the peasants. Glancing nervously at the cat, the peasants replied, "The Marquis of Carabas owns all these fields."

"Well," said the king, "we've seen your vast forest, and now we see your fine fields."

The miller's son nodded, not knowing quite what to say. But the princess took his silence for modesty, and smiled.

Puss in Boots ran ahead of the carriage until he came to an enormous castle. The castle was owned by a dreaded ogre, who also owned all the land along the road. The cat trotted through the gate.

Upon his request, Puss in Boots was escorted to the ogre's chamber. "Pardon me," said the cat, removing his hat with a flourish. "I had to make your acquaintance, having heard tell of your fame far and wide."

The ogre was flattered, but replied gruffly, "I've no time for vanities. What is it you want?"

"I cannot believe stories that you can transform yourself into anything you want," said the cat.

"I shall prove I can do just that!" thundered the ogre. "And then you shall die for doubting my powers."

Before Puss in Boots could
say another word, the ogre
turned himself into a ferocious
lion. The ogre's words dissolved
into angry roars, as he waved
his huge paw in the air,
brandishing his sharp claws.

Puss was frightened nearly out of his boots. "If you please!" he shouted, to be heard above the roars. "That *is* amazing. But I doubt you could change yourself into something as small as, say, a mouse." No sooner had he spoken the words, then the vain ogre turned himself into a tiny fieldmouse. "Splendid!" cried Puss, clapping his paws together.

"And now I shall eat you!" cried the cat. As quick as a wink, Puss in Boots caught the mouse and ate him in one bite. Then he put on his hat, cleaned his whiskers, and made his way about the castle, sternly informing all the servants that they were soon to meet their new master.

Soon the royal carriage arrived, for the castle stood at the end of the road. Puss in Boots greeted the royal party at the gate. "Welcome to the castle of the Marquis of Carabas!" he exclaimed. "Perhaps you'd like some refreshment after your journey."

The king was delighted
that his new friend, of whom
his daughter appeared to be
very fond, lived in such a
splendid castle.

"My house is your house,"
said the young man humbly.

The young man and the princess felt love growing between them as they gazed at each other. Holding hands, they walked dreamily up the castle steps with the king.

Puss in Boots smiled. "Catching mice can be of great use," the cat said to himself.

The group went into the Great Hall, where
a cold banquet had been quickly prepared
by order of the cat. The king proposed
that the marquis marry his daughter, and
the happy couple agreed.

173

A lavish wedding was planned for the marquis and the princess, who were so obviously in love. No one in the kingdom could doubt that it was a joyous event, for all the bells in the land rang out the good tidings. Lords and peasants alike were invited to the wedding, in which Puss in Boots played a part by proudly holding the princess's train.

At the wedding the new prince promised his brothers land and wealth. When they asked how he had come to such success, he winked and replied, "Great fortunes can be made with a cat."

As for Puss in Boots, he found the comforts of castle living to his liking, and he lived happily ever after.

"VAN GOOL'S"

# Hansel and Gretel

A poor woodcutter and his wife lived in a small cottage with their two children, a boy named Hansel, and his sister, Gretel. One night, the children overheard their parents talking in the kitchen. There was a great famine in the land. The family had little food left and no money. "We must take the children, and go deep into the woods to search for food," said the father in a worried tone, "or else we will all starve."

Gretel was alarmed, as they had never ventured deep into the woods before. "Don't worry," said Hansel. "I'll drop some pebbles along the path so we can find our way home." The next morning, as they set off, Hansel began to lay the trail.

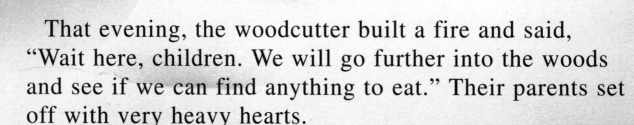

That evening, the woodcutter built a fire and said, "Wait here, children. We will go further into the woods and see if we can find anything to eat." Their parents set off with very heavy hearts.

Hansel and Gretel watched
them disappear among the trees.
Then they lay down beside
the fire and fell asleep.

When the fire was only a pile of ashes, the children woke up cold and hungry. Their parents had been gone a long time. "What shall we do, Hansel?" sobbed Gretel. "Wait until the moon comes out," he said cheerfully, "and by its light, we will follow the pebbles back home."

When the moon rose in the sky, they made their way back to the path. In the bright light, they soon found the pebbles.

"Look, here's one," cried Gretel. "And another!" They began their journey home.

By dawn, they were back at the clearing where their cottage stood. They ran into the house, calling, "Father, Mother, we're home!"

Their father was so glad to see them. In the dark, he had missed the path back to the children and was setting out to search for them. Happy to be together again, they forgot about their problems...
for a short while.

But soon after, the crops failed again and the woodcutter told his wife, "We must return to the forest, and look for food. "When Gretel heard this she told Hansel to go out and collect some pebbles, just in case they got lost again.
But it was late at night, and the door to the cottage was locked!

In the morning, their mother gave them each a piece of bread, the last in the house. "Eat yours," Hansel whispered to Gretel, "and I will drop the crumbs from mine on the path." Trailing behind the others, Hansel threw down crumbs to mark their way.

But he forgot about the birds, who were also hungry. They swooped down to the path and ate up all this crumbs.

While Hansel and Gretel were playing in the woods, they lost sight of their parents. Unconcerned, they tried to retrace their steps, but couldn't find a single crumb to guide them.

"Never mind, Hansel," said Gretel bravely, "we shall just have to find our own way home."

The children walked for a long time.
They were tired and hungry when,
suddenly, a magnificent white peacock
appeared before them.

"Follow me," she screeched.

The bird led Hansel and Gretel to a clearing in the forest, where they found a wonderful little house made of sweets and cake! "Oh!" they cried, unable to believe their eyes.

At once, the children began to pull off pieces of the shutters and to pick the lollipop flowers.
They were alarmed when they heard a shrill voice call from inside:

*Nibble, nibble, like a mouse,*
*Who is nibbling at my house?*

"It's only the wind," answered Hansel and Gretel nervously, eating as fast as they could.

But they stopped in fright when an ugly old woman came out and beckoned to them. They were about to run away when she said sweetly, "Why don't you come in for a while?" Unwisely, Hansel and Gretel followed her into the house.

Although she pretended to be kind, the old woman was really a wicked witch, who liked to eat children.
But she put Hansel and Gretel at ease by offering them a splendid feast.

The witch set the table with more food than the children had ever seen. There were pastries and cakes, chocolates and sweets, delicious drinks - everything you could imagine. Hansel and Gretel spent all afternoon eating until they were so full they could eat no more.

The witch sent them to bed, and returned to the kitchen to plot and scheme.

"They are thin," she said to herself. "But if I feed the boy large meals, he will soon be fat enough to eat. And then I'll deal with his sister."

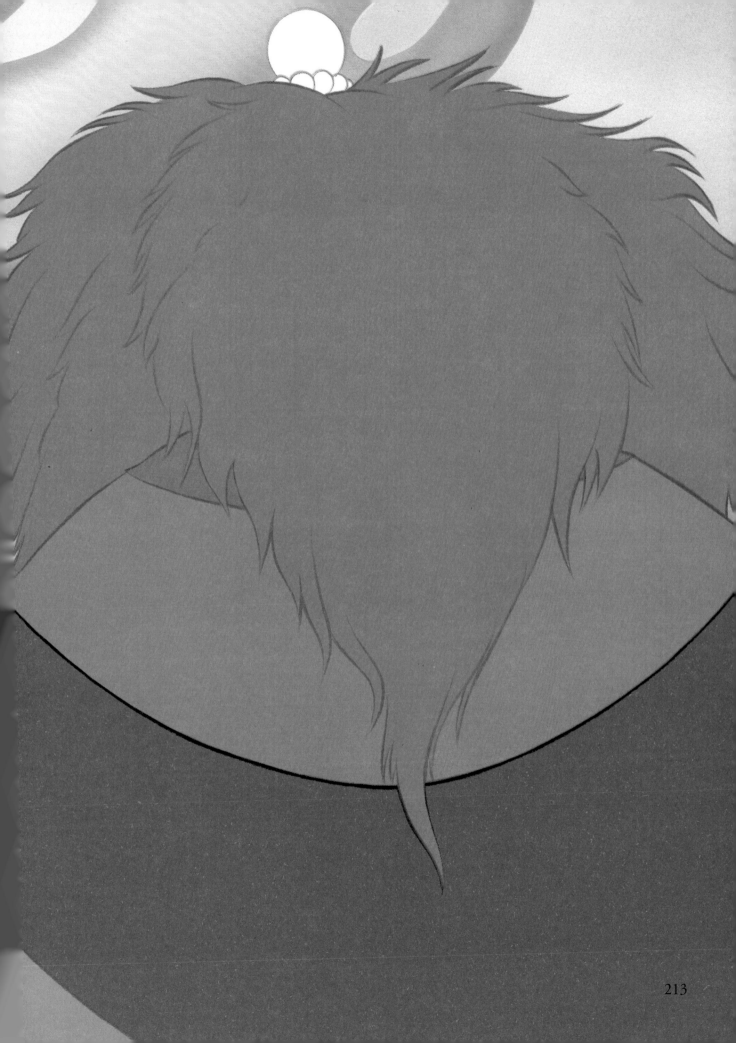

The next morning, the cruel witch pulled Hansel from his bed and locked him in a cage in the cellar. "And there you'll stay," she cackled, "until you're fat enough to eat. Meanwhile, your sister can do all the housework!"

"Let me go!" cried the frightened boy.
But the witch paid no attention to his cries.

The witch woke Gretel, saying, "Fetch water from the stream and clean the house! You are also to cook a large meal every day for your brother, until he is fat enough for me to eat!" Gretel was terrified, but she had no choice. So she started her chores.

Gretel worked hard, but the cruel witch
gave her only scraps to eat. These she shared
with the mice who came to the table.
All the time she thought only of how she
could free Hansel so they could both escape.

Every day, the witch visited Hansel. "Stick your finger through the bars so I can tell how fat you're getting," she said. (She was so short-sighted she could hardly see.) But Hansel was clever, and stuck a chicken bone through the bars. The witch pinched it, thinking it was his finger, and couldn't understand why he wasn't growing fatter.

After several weeks, the witch lost patience. "Fat or thin, I will eat him today!" she declared. She handed Gretel a bundle of sticks and told her to build a fire in the oven. Gretel knew this was her only chance!

When the fire was blazing, she asked the witch, "How can I tell if the oven is hot enough?"

"Like this, you foolish girl," snapped the witch, and she bent over the oven to feel the heat. In an instant, Gretel had pushed the witch into the oven and slammed the door tightly shut!

"Hansel! We're free!" she cried happily, running to unlock the cage. "The witch is dead!" The children hugged each other tightly and danced around the room.

Then they went and searched the cottage, looking for the witch's hidden treasures - sparkling jewels she had stolen from other people who had also lost their way in the woods. They filled two sacks with precious stones. They had found a fortune!

"Now, let's get away from here!"
cried Hansel. And they ran out into
the forest searching for a way home.
Finally, they found a stream they knew.
But it was too wide to wade or swim
across.

Gretel spotted a beautiful white swan out on the water. She called:

*Swan, swan, here we stand,*
*Hansel and Gretel, on the land,*
*Stepping stones and bridge we lack,*
*Please carry us over on your white back.*

The swan kindly came to the bank of the stream and, in turn, took them across the water. They were now close to home.

Their father had just come out of the cottage to chop wood when Hansel and Gretel ran into his arms. He was overjoyed to see them alive and well. He had searched the whole countryside for news of them.

"Come and see what we've brought home!" cried Hansel excitedly.

The children tipped the sacks of precious stones onto the table, and their father picked one up in wonder.

"We'll never be poor or no hungry again!"
said Hansel. "Mother, come quickly!"
Their mother came to join them and they all
danced for joy!

# Pinocchio

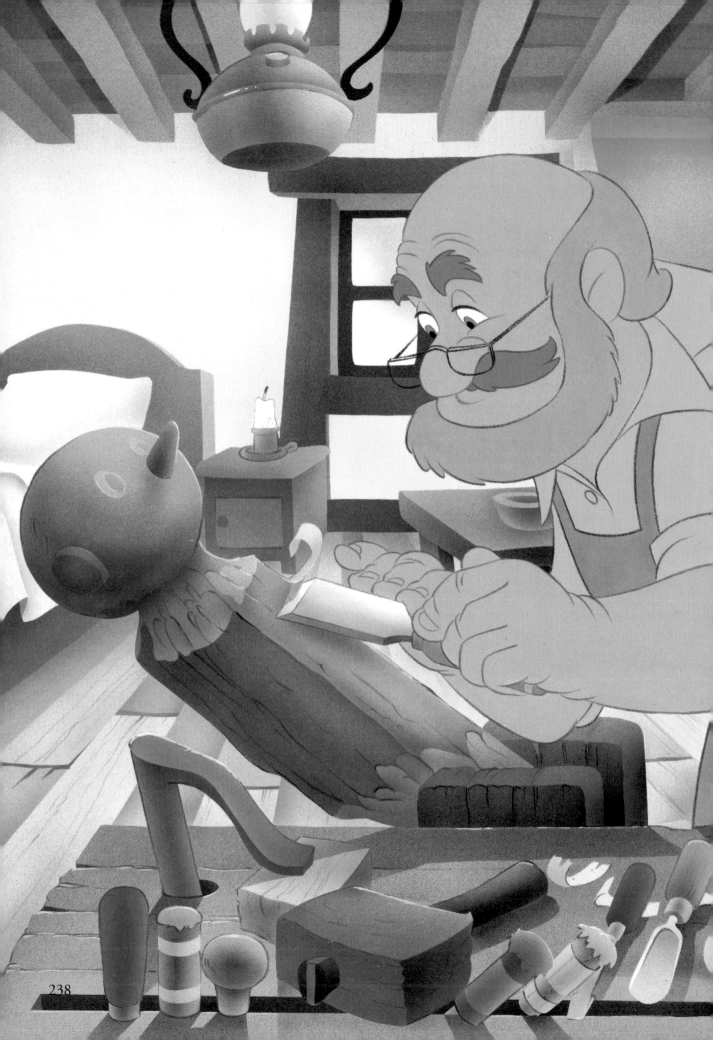

One day Geppetto, a woodcarver, decided to carve a little boy puppet. As he worked he thought of a name for his creation - Pinocchio.

No sooner had Geppetto made the puppet's eyes, than they looked around the room, then stared at him. Then Geppetto made a nose. Next Geppetto made a mouth, which sang and laughed.

Quickly then, Geppetto finished carving the body, and attached the arms and legs. When Pinocchio was placed on the floor he fell into a heap.

"This is how to walk, little Pinocchio," said Geppetto. He led Pinocchio by the hand, showing him how to place one foot in front of the other. Soon Pinocchio could walk without help. Then the spirited puppet dashed away down the street.

"Come back!" cried Geppetto, but Pinocchio did not listen.

As he raced and danced through the streets, Pinocchio's feet clattered on the cobblestones. Finally, Geppetto caught Pinocchio by the nose, and said angrily, "Come home with me, where I will teach you a lesson!"

Thinking Geppetto was a bully, two policemen seized him and took the poor man to jail.

Pinocchio didn't feel at all sorry that he had caused Geppetto such trouble. The little puppet returned home. Suddenly, he heard a voice. "*Cri-cri-cri.* Learn to be good."

"Who said that?" asked Pinocchio, frightened.

"It's me, the cricket," answered the voice.

Pinocchio saw an enormous cricket sitting on the mantlepiece. "A cricket! What are you doing here?"

"I live here," said the cricket. "And I have to tell you, that you should learn to listen and to be kind to others."

"Oh, be quiet!" shouted Pinocchio rudely.

By now it was dark outside, and Pinocchio was hungry. He searched the room but could not find a scrap of food. About to give up, Pinocchio finally found an egg. But when the eager puppet tried to crack the egg into a pan, a chick popped out, ran off the table, and flew out the window.

The hungry puppet went into the village and banged on a door. A grumpy man in a nightshirt came to the window. "What do you want? It's late!" he shouted.

"Please, would you give me a piece of bread?" asked Pinocchio.

"Wait here," replied the man. He thought Pinocchio was playing a trick on him. He returned to the window and threw water on the poor puppet, drenching him from head to toe.

Now Pinocchio was wet, as well as tired and hungry. He ran home and sat on a stool. To warm his feet he put them on the hearth, too close to the fire, and fell asleep at once. But while he slept, his little wooden feet caught fire, and smouldered to ashes.

In the morning Pinocchio was awakened by a loud banging at the door.

"It's Geppetto! Open up!" shouted an angry voice.

But when Pinocchio jumped to unlock the door, he fell flat. Geppetto had to climb in through the window.

Geppetto was furious at having been thrown in jail on Pinocchio's account, but when he saw his little puppet lying helplessly with no feet, his heart softened. He carved a fine pair of little feet and attached them to Pinocchio's legs.

"Now don't run away on these new feet!" cautioned Geppetto.

"I won't, papa," replied Pinocchio. "I'll try to do things right, now. I'll even go to school."

"That's a good boy," said Geppetto proudly.

Then Pinocchio tucked a book under his arm and started out for school.

Pinocchio talked to himself as he walked. "This time," he said, "I'll do just as papa says. I'll go to school and learn to read and write."

But Pinocchio began to hear music, and he stopped to listen. Then, forgetting about school, he followed the sound until he came to a puppet show, surrounded by a crowd of people.

The show was so funny and lively that soon Pinocchio was laughing with everyone else. His delight and excitement grew until, carried away, he leaped onto the stage. The stringless puppet drew such a thunderous applause for his antics that when the show ended the puppeteer gave Pinocchio five gold pieces. "Give them to your father," he said.

Pinocchio happily set off for home, but a fox and cat stopped him on the way.

"I'm going home to give my gold coins to my papa," Pinocchio told them.

Thinking quickly, the sly fox said, "I know how you can turn those five coins into five hundred! Come along with us."

At first, Pinocchio objected, saying his papa was waiting for him. But the thought of five hundred gold coins danced in his head, and he soon agreed to join the fox and cat. They brought him to an inn, where they feasted royally, using one of Pinocchio's coins, and explained the plan.

"You plant your coins in the Field of Miracles," said the fox. "And in the morning you'll find a tree, laden with more coins than you can count!"

253

Their plan was to sleep at the inn until midnight, then go and plant the coins. The tired Pinocchio fell deep asleep, and dreamed of trees full of gold coins, tinkling in the breeze. But when Pinocchio awoke, his friends were gone.

"I will find the Field of Miracles myself," thought the puppet. "Maybe my friends are waiting for me there."

Taking the four gold coins he had left, Pinocchio set off down the path. He was surprised to meet the talking cricket along the way.

"I'm here to give you some advice," said the cricket. "Go home now to poor Geppetto, and give him your coins. He's terribly sad because he misses you."

"But tomorrow my papa will be rich!" said the puppet.

Pinocchio would not listen to the cricket, and continued on his way. He was busy thinking of things he would buy with his money, when he heard footsteps behind him. Pinocchio turned to look, and saw two figures, about the same size as the fox and the cat, wearing masks and following him. As he began to run, they chased after him.

Pinocchio ran for miles, the masked figures close behind. He was ready to drop with exhaustion when he saw a house far in the distance. He dashed toward the house. A blue-haired woman stood at the window.

"Help!" cried Pinocchio. "They're after me!"

But then the masked figures caught him. "Your money or your life," said one of them gruffly. But Pinocchio couldn't speak because he had the coins under his tongue.

"Alright then," said the other, "we'll fix him!"

They hanged poor Pinocchio in a tree, but when he didn't die right away they grew tired of waiting. "We'll come back tomorrow," said one of them as they left.

Pinocchio hanged for a long time. He hoped someone would save him. He thought of his papa, and wished he had listened to the cricket. Then the puppet closed his eyes. He didn't see the animal servants of the blue-haired woman coming to take him from the tree. They brought Pinocchio to her house, where the woman gently placed him on a bed.

"Is he alive?" asked the owl.

"I don't know," replied the blue-haired woman, who was really a kind fairy. Just then Pinocchio began to shiver and shake.

"I know that puppet," said the cricket. "He is a naughty rascal who won't listen, and will make his poor papa die of a broken heart."

When the animals left the room, the Blue Fairy asked, "Why aren't you home with your papa, like a good boy?"

"It's not my fault," said Pinocchio. "The cat and fox made me go with them." As soon as Pinocchio said this, his nose began to grow.

"Your lie is as plain as the nose on your face," laughed the Fairy.

"Please fix my nose!" cried the puppet. "I promise not to lie again."

Pinocchio's nose returned to its normal size. He thanked the Fairy for her help, and set off to go straight home to his papa. But when he approached the hanging tree, he saw the fox and cat.

"Ah, Pinocchio! Are you ready now to go to the Field of Miracles?" called the fox.

"Why did you disappear from the inn last night? When I tried to find the field, two robbers tried to kill me," said Pinocchio.

"We had to see a sick relative," lied the cat.

"But we're together again!" exclaimed the fox. And they convinced the puppet to go with them to the Field of Miracles, where he planted his coins.

"We must be going, now," said the fox.

"Good luck to you," said the cat.

"Good-bye, and thank you!" called Pinocchio as they left. Then he lay down happily on the ground, and fell fast asleep, dreaming again of riches.

When Pinocchio awoke, his gold was gone. "Where are all my coins?" he wondered aloud.

"Gone! Long gone!" answered a parrot, perched in the tree nearby. "The cat and fox dug them up while you slept, and ran away."

Pinocchio's mouth dropped open. He began to cry.

Sad and ashamed, Pinocchio decided to return to the Blue Fairy, who had been so kind to him. He ran back along the path, but when at last he came to where the house had stood, there was only a gravestone in its place.

Pinocchio fell to his knees and sobbed.

"Come back, Blue Fairy!" he lamented.

Just then an enormous pigeon landed nearby. "Have you seen a puppet named Pinocchio?" asked the bird.

"I'm Pinocchio!" answered the puppet.

"Come with me, then," said the pigeon. "Geppetto is setting out to sea to look for you."

Pinocchio dried his tears, climbed onto the pigeon's back, and away they flew.

The pigeon and Pinocchio travelled all day, and then all night, before reaching the coast. Pinocchio slid off the pigeon's back, but when he turned to thank him, the kind bird had already flown away. The little puppet looked across the wide stretch of blue ocean, and caught sight of a little boat with a man in it, bobbing in the waves.

"Papa!" screamed Pinocchio. But just then a big wave swamped the boat, which disappeared. "I'll save you!" shouted the puppet, diving into the sea. Pinocchio swam for a long time, and just when he thought his strength would desert him, he reached an island. A dolphin told him that Geppetto had been swallowed by a huge shark.

"What shall I do now?" moaned Pinocchio.
"First the Blue Fairy, now Geppetto! I'm all
alone." But before Pinocchio could feel too
terribly sad, he realized that he was very, very
hungry. "This must lead somewhere," he
thought, setting off on a path.

Before long he met an old woman carrying a
water jug, and he offered to carry her jug if she
would give him some bread and water.

At the woman's house
Pinocchio ate his fill. When he
looked up from his plate, he
saw that the old woman had
changed into the Blue Fairy.
"You're alive! You're here!"
shouted Pinocchio joyfully.

After they hugged, the Blue
Fairy told Pinocchio she
would care for him like a
mother. He promised to try
very hard to be good.

The next day Pinocchio went to school, and the day after, and the day after that. He studied his books, he listened to the Blue Fairy, and helped with the chores. But one day on the way to school, the boys told Pinocchio they were going to see a great shark in the ocean near the beach. Pinocchio thought of Geppetto, and decided to join the boys.

But when they reached the sea, no shark could be seen. When the boys began to laugh, Pinocchio realized they had tricked him. The boys began to fight.

Then a boy hit on the head by a book fell to the ground. The other boys ran away. Pinocchio stayed to help the hurt boy. But when a policeman came and accused Pinocchio, he ran away in fear.

It was dark when the frightened puppet made his way back to the village, and knocked on the Blue Fairy's door. A snail poked its head out the window.

"I'm Pinocchio! Let me in!" cried the puppet.

It took the snail, being as slow as all snails are, until morning to open the door. While he waited, Pinocchio had lots of time to think of how his naughtiness brought nothing but trouble.

Pinocchio decided to change. In the weeks that followed
he behaved well, and went to school every day. One day the
Blue Fairy announced, "Pinocchio, you are ready at last.
Tomorrow your great wish will come true. You'll turn into a
real boy! Let's have a party to celebrate. You may go to
invite your friends, but come back before dark."

Pinocchio set off to invite his friends. But when he invited his mischievous friend, Lampwick, the boy replied, "Well, good luck to you, Pinocchio. I can't come though, because I'm running away to Funland. The wagon is coming to pick me up tonight, with all the other boys. Every day is a holiday in Funland, filled with games, rides and sweets!"

Although Pinocchio tried to resist, when the wagon appeared, loaded with happy boys and pulled by donkeys, Lampwick and the coachman convinced the wayward puppet to join them.

All the way to Funland, Pinocchio thought of the Blue Fairy, and how he had behaved so well that she was going to make him a real boy. "I'll go home tomorrow," he thought. But as soon as he and Lampwick were in Funland, they were carried away by the endless games and sweets. Suddenly one day the boys were horrified to see that they had grown donkey ears.

Before long the miserable boys had changed completely into donkeys, for that was the fate of all boys in Funland. The cruel coachman then sold Pinocchio to a circus, where the ringmaster taught the donkey tricks. On his first night performing, Pinocchio sprained both his front legs so badly that he couldn't walk.

"I've paid good money for you," growled the ringmaster. "And now you're no good to me at all!" The man tied a heavy rock to Pinocchio's neck and pushed him over a cliff into the sea.

But the seawater magically changed the donkey into a puppet again and the rock slipped from his neck. Pinocchio swam away from the shore.

"What a close call!" thought Pinocchio. But his troubles were not over, for suddenly an enormous shark appeared. "Help!" cried Pinocchio. As he flailed in the water, the monstrous shark opened its cavernous mouth.

Pinocchio swam as fast as he could, but the shark was faster. It caught up with Pinocchio and sucked him into a whirlpool of water that plunged down into the shark's belly.

It was dark and wet in the shark's belly.
"Help!" cried Pinocchio. "Oh, poor me!"
"Who is that?" asked a voice.
Pinocchio's despair turned suddenly to joy, for
there, floating in his little boat, was Geppetto.

After their tearful reunion, Pinocchio said, "Papa, we must escape from this awful place."

"But how?" asked Geppetto. "I don't know how to swim."

"I can help, if you show me the way," came a voice. Beside them surfaced a tunafish that had been swallowed in the same gulp with Pinocchio. The two climbed on the fish's back and made their way through the shark's throat and out through his mouth, which was open as he slept.

Geppetto and Pinocchio rode comfortably on the tuna's back until they reached land. Then they thanked the helpful fish, and bade him good-bye.

Pinocchio helped his weak and trembling papa home, carrying him much of the way. Once there, he tucked Geppetto in bed and fed him hot soup. "I will take care of you now," said Pinocchio. "I will go to school, and I'll work to make money for us to live on."

"Pinocchio, you are so changed!" exclaimed Geppetto.

Pinocchio worked hard from that day on, doing his studies and his chores, and weaving baskets to make money for food. Geppetto slowly began to get better, and they shared many happy moments together. Then one day, the Blue Fairy appeared. "Brave, kind Pinocchio!" she said. "With your tender care and hard work, you have proved that your heart is good."

"You deserve to become a real boy now," said the Fairy with a smile.

With a cry of delight, Pinocchio found that he was no longer a wooden puppet, but a real live boy. He ran to embrace Geppetto.

"My son," said Geppetto. "It is a happy day indeed!"

"VAN GOOL'S"

# Sleeping Beauty

A very many years ago there lived a king and queen. Together they ruled wisely over their kingdom. Although they loved each other, they couldn't feel completely happy because they wanted very much to have a child. Their pet dog, Jester, brought them some happiness, but at night, when the dog and all the servants were asleep, the king and queen would sigh and wish for a child to brighten their castle.

One day the king and queen's dearest wish came true, and the queen gave birth to a lovely baby girl. The king danced merrily about the room, then rushed to his daughter's side. "You are so beautiful and precious!" he exclaimed to the sleeping baby. "We must have a royal party to invite all the fairies of the kingdom to meet you and share our happiness!"

The day was set for the party, the invitations went out, the royal cooks prepared a feast, and all was ready. On the day of the party the fairies flew into the castle, by various means, to celebrate the birth of the baby.

After the fairies peered into the cradle to see the sleeping baby, they took their seats at the banquet table. The king lifted his glass. "To a long and happy life for our little princess!" he proclaimed. The guests cheered and clapped.

Everyone at the party enjoyed the delicious feast, then danced to the music of a lively band. The king even danced with his baby in his arms. Then he gave each of the fairies a box of glittering jewels to thank them for coming.

But the joyful celebration was interrupted when the ballroom doors flew open and a scowling figure stormed across the floor. It was the evil and most powerful fairy of the kingdom. The king and queen had quite forgotten to invite her to the party. She glared angrily at the innocent baby, then turned to the other fairies. "Go ahead and give the child your gifts," she said. "And then I shall give mine!"

307

The king and queen and the fairies tried to carry on with the party, although the wicked fairy had spoiled the happy mood. One by one the fairies approached the baby princess, and bestowed their happy wishes. The smallest fairy hid behind the cradle.

Then the evil fairy stalked across the room. She scooped up the baby in her enormous hand, and as she bestowed her evil spell, the baby appeared as the beautiful woman she would become. "When you have grown to a young woman," uttered the fairy, "you will prick your thumb on a spindle, and will die!"

After the evil fairy stalked out of the castle, the smallest fairy stepped forward. "The evil fairy is so powerful that I cannot erase the spell, but I can soften it," she said. "Princess, when the spindle pricks your thumb you will not die, but shall sleep for a hundred years. After that only a prince's kiss may awaken you."

The king and queen were determined to protect their child from harm. The king sent his heralds throughout the kingdom, where they issued his royal proclamation that all spinning wheels be brought to the castle courtyard and burned.

The years passed and the baby grew into a lovely young woman. Her heart was kind and good, and she was loved by all. The king and queen had never told her of the evil fairy's spell. One day they set out to tour the kingdom, leaving the princess and Jester with the castle servants.

The princess, who loved to explore the castle, was delighted to discover a stairway she had never seen before.

Dreamily, she made her way up the stairs. The sunlight dissolved into a gloomy darkness at the top of the stairs, where a wooden door was shut tight. The curious princess could hear something on the other side of the door, and as she peeked through the keyhole and leaned against the door, it swung open.

In the cold, dark room on the other side of the door, an old woman, hidden in a cloak, sat spinning by candlelight. The princess watched, transfixed, for she had never seen a spinning wheel. Jester whimpered.

"Come closer," invited the woman. "Would you like to try it?"

The princess slowly crossed the room.

"Here, take this spindle," crooned the woman. But as the princess reached for the spindle, the sharp point pricked her thumb. At once sleepiness overcame the princess, who fell to her knees. The woman pushed back her hood, revealing the frightening face of the evil fairy.

Later that day, when the king and queen returned from their trip, their beloved daughter did not run out to greet them. Jester led them to the tower room, where they found their daughter on the floor by the spinning wheel. Sadly they lay the princess on her bed.

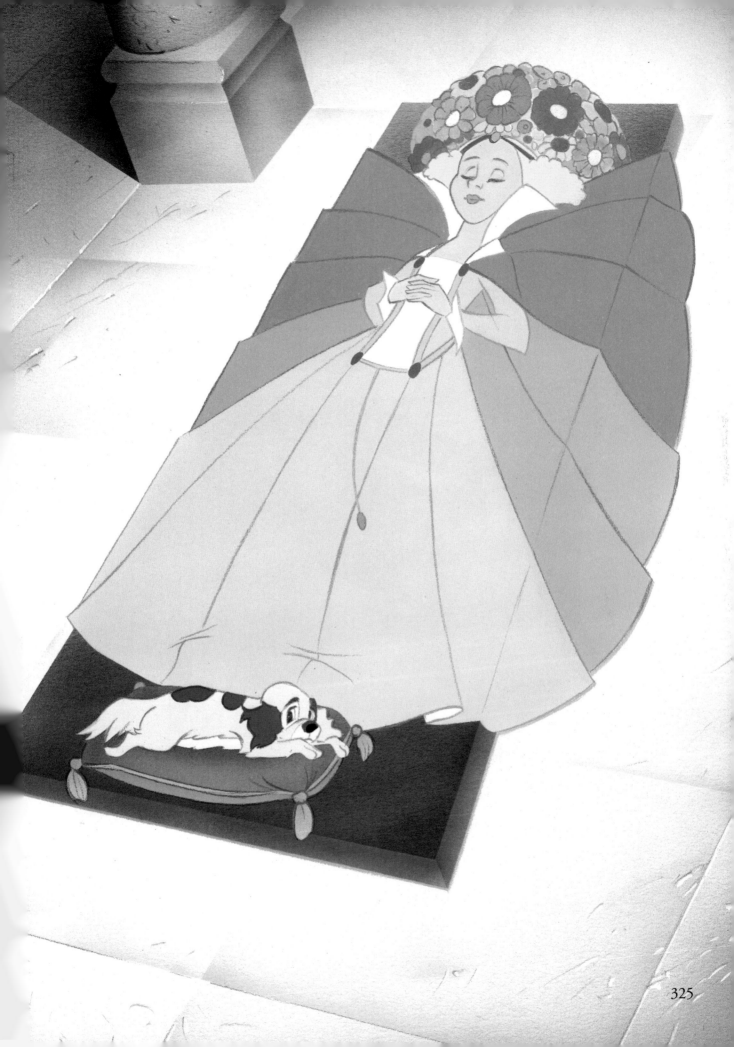

Then the queen ordered the royal messenger, with his seven-league boots, to summon the smallest fairy to the castle. The messenger bounded across the kingdom until he found the fairy. Then, wiping a tear from his face, he said, "You must come quickly! The princess has fallen under an evil spell."

With her pet birds pulling the hem of her long dress, and the messenger balanced in her skirt, she flew to the castle. There she found the princess, grown to a woman and deep in a dreamless sleep, watched over by her unhappy parents.

The fairy flitted throughout the castle, casting a magic spell that put everyone into a deep slumber. The cooks with their pots and pans, the maids with their sewing and cleaning, the grooms with their horses, the butler in his pantry . . .

. . . the guards at the entrance, the ladies in waiting – everyone was soon fast asleep.

"Now no one will age during the princess's long sleep," said the fairy.

Night came, then day, and nothing changed. A week passed, then a month, then years came and went, and still all slumbered on under the enchantment. The trees grew, and vines climbed the castle walls. A hundred years passed.

One day a prince from the nearby kingdom got lost in the mountains. He spied a castle in the distant woods, then came upon a peasant in his field, who told him the story of the sleeping princess. "But no one can enter that castle," he finished. "It is all grown over with brambles."

The prince decided to see for himself. "Surely it can't be true," he said to his horse. "I heard that story long ago. It's only a fairy tale!"

As the prince approached the castle, the thorny brambles flattened themselves to the ground by some strange magic. The prince walked over them with ease.

As soon as the prince pushed open the castle door, and stepped inside, he knew that the story was true. In every room people were frozen deep in sleep, wearing old-fashioned clothes and covered with dust and cobwebs.

The prince wandered through the castle until he came to the room of the slumbering princess. Sadly, he knelt by her bed. "You are a sleeping beauty," he whispered, overcome by her loveliness. Then he gave her a gentle kiss.

The princess sighed, then opened her eyes. "Who are you?" she asked. The prince told her who he was, and how he had come to be there, and the story of the fairy's wicked spell. While he spoke, the princess listened in wonder, and felt love growing in her heart.

When the prince had broken the spell with his kiss, everyone in the castle had also come to life. The king and queen rushed to their daughter's bed, where they were overjoyed to find the princess awake, and delighted to meet the prince who had ended the enchantment.

And it was decreed that on the seventh day the prince and princess would be married. Invitations were sent out to friends and family, and to the fairies of the kingdom. The king and queen noted, with satisfaction, the tenderness and love shared by the young couple.

All the kingdom rejoiced when the princess and prince were married. After the ceremony, lively music and dancing filled the castle with the merriest sounds in a hundred years. And the princess and prince lived together, in love and happiness, ever after.